THIS BOOK BELONGS TO

To Dave, who has loved me through everything
— Sarah Lowes

To my dear princes
— Miss Clara

THE SNOW QUEEN

Retold by **Sarah Lowes**
Illustrated by **Miss Clara**
Narrated by **Xanthe Gresham**

Barefoot Books
step inside a story

Contents

The Mirror and its Fragments

Listen! The story begins. Perhaps, by the end, we shall know more than we do now. There was once a magician who delighted in the dark side of his magical arts. One day, he invented a remarkable mirror. This mirror made ugly things look huge and shrank beautiful ones almost to nothing. The beauty of this world disappeared altogether in the mirror's glass and plain things appeared ten times drearier than before. Lush green fields looked like boiled spinach, and people who were usually quite attractive and pleasant became so ugly and hateful that even their friends couldn't recognize them. A girl with just one pimple looked as though it had spread all over her face, and if she had a good or a happy thought, a wrinkle immediately appeared in the mirror.

The magician's apprentices revelled in the misery that the mirror created, and they flew around the world with it until there was no one left who had not gazed into it. Everyone turned aside in horror at their hideous reflections, or at the sight of the cruelty and vice that the mirror displayed.

One day, the apprentices brought the mirror to the Snow Queen. She knew at once that the mirror would be her perfect weapon against happiness and contentment, and she formed a plan. She commanded the apprentices to fly up into the sky with the mirror.

As they did so, the mirror began to crack until it shattered into millions of tiny pieces, and the Queen laughed with a cruel joy at what would come next.

The splinters of glass scattered themselves all over the world and continued their evil work. Some pieces were large enough to be made into windowpanes, making the view from those houses a sorry sight indeed. Smaller fragments were used to make spectacles, causing their owners endless trouble as they tried to see clearly through them. Little bits of the mirror were set into rings. Tiny pieces slipped into some people's eyes, making everything they looked upon seem ugly and hopeless. Worst by far was the fate of those who received a splinter of glass in their hearts: people who had once been warm and loving became cold and hard.

Fragments of that mirror exist to this very day. Others play a part in my story, as will soon be revealed.

CHAPTER TWO

A Little Boy and a Little Girl

In the poorest part of a large town, a boy and girl called Kay and Gerda lived opposite each other with their families. Outside each house was a wooden trough in which herbs, flowers and a rose tree grew. The two trees grew up and intertwined, forming an arch between the houses. In the summer, Kay and Gerda would sit under its blooms and play or read for hours at a time.

A cold, snowy winter came and one of the children's favorite games was to heat a penny on their stoves and press it to the frozen windowpane. A little circle of ice would melt and each child would look out with a bright, gentle eye at the other across the street. On very cold days, they would sit by the stove in Gerda's house and her grandmother

would tell them a story. One afternoon she told Kay and Gerda about the Snow Queen. "She passes by each house at night," she told them, "and breathes on the windowpanes, leaving frosty patterns behind."

Kay's eyes grew wide when he heard this. That night, he opened his bedroom window and looked out. The snow was falling silently, and as he watched, one snowflake seemed to grow in size until it became a dazzling figure. The figure was of a woman, dressed all in white. She was tall and beautiful, with eyes like glittering stars and a crown made of twinkling icicles. The woman looked at Kay with her shining eyes and beckoned him to join her, but he was afraid and drew back. She smiled and blew him a kiss and with it two splinters of the magic mirror. One entered his eye and the other, his heart. For a moment, Kay felt a stinging sensation and then all was just as before.

The days went by and Kay became more and more grumpy and discontented. Everything that had previously brought him joy now seemed dull and uninteresting. He told Gerda that her favorite picture book was for babies and that the rose arch was ugly. Kay argued and interrupted when Gerda's grandmother tried to tell them a story and even mimicked her and other neighbors when they weren't looking. The splinters of mirror in his eye and heart made him quite unmoved by the sufferings of others. He did not even care when he hurt Gerda's feelings. His heart was slowly turning to ice, freezing out any feelings of happiness and compassion, and he found himself yearning for something he could not name.

Kay stopped playing with Gerda and took to going skating with the bigger boys instead. One day he decided to join them as they hitched their sledges to passing sleighs. He fastened his sledge to the biggest, finest sleigh he could find and set off for a free ride, feeling very pleased with himself.

At first it was fun speeding through the streets, listening to the swish of the runners as they hissed along. Soon, however, the sleigh left the town and set out for the open countryside. Kay wanted to go back as it would soon be nightfall, but try as he might, he could not unhitch his sledge.

He cried out in alarm and tried to attract the attention of the sleigh driver, but the falling snow was turning into a blizzard and the wind muffled his cries. Further and further from home they sped, with Kay clinging to his sledge, bitterly cold. He began to feel sleepy, and through his half-closed eyes, the snowflakes looked like big white birds, flying all around him. Then, all at once, the sleigh stopped and the driver turned around. It was the Snow Queen.

"My poor frozen one," she said in a voice like tinkling icicles, "come and sit under my fur wrap." Kay climbed stiffly into her beautiful sleigh and sat close beside her. She bent to kiss his forehead and her kiss was as cold as ice. Kay felt as though his blood had frozen at her touch. Yet when he looked into her face, it seemed to him as though there was no more beautiful or enchanting person in all the world. She sparkled like pure, ice-cold perfection. As the sleigh flew up into the dark night sky, all thoughts of home and Gerda vanished.

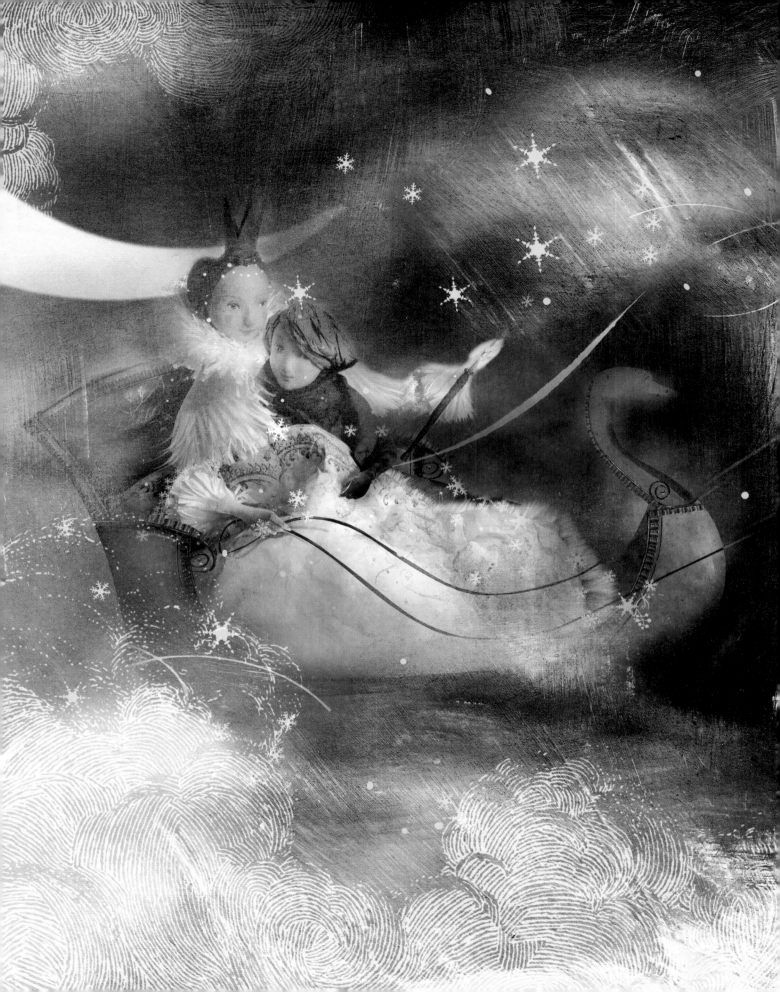

CHAPTER THREE

The Enchanted Flower Garden

Gerda was very anxious when Kay did not come home that night. The big boys said that they had seen him hitch his sledge to a beautiful white sleigh and drive out of the town gates. Days and weeks went by and still he didn't return. Kay's family mourned his absence and Gerda shed many lonely tears.

When spring came, Gerda looked at the first golden rays of the sun as they warmed the new buds on the rose arch. "Kay is dead," she whispered.

"I doubt that," said the sun, gleaming softly. Some sparrows hopped towards her, hoping for some crumbs of bread.

"Kay is dead," she said sadly.

"We doubt that," twittered the sparrows. Then all at once, Gerda doubted it too.

"I will put on my red shoes and I will go and find him and bring him home," she said to herself firmly and set off for the river.

At the riverbank, she called out: "Have you seen Kay? If I give you my new red shoes, will you send him back to me?" The river didn't reply, but it seemed to the lonely girl that it was listening to her in a kindly and inviting way, so she took off her shoes and threw them into its fast-flowing waters.

When the little wavelets brought them back to her, however, Gerda thought she hadn't thrown them far enough. She climbed into a boat and, gathering all her strength, hurled the shoes out into the river once more. As she did so, the boat began to glide away from the shore with Gerda still on board. She was very much frightened at first, but as there was nothing she could do to stop it, she settled down to look at the scenery. The sparrows flew alongside her companionably and her red shoes floated behind the boat. "Perhaps the river is taking me to see Kay," thought Gerda, and she resolved to enjoy herself as best she could.

After a while, she sailed past a cottage with red and blue windows and two fine rose bushes at the door. She saw a garden full of beautiful flowers with an old woman in a sunbonnet weeding by the river's edge. Gerda called to her and the old woman used her walking stick to pull the boat into the bank. She helped Gerda out of the boat and invited her into her cottage for a rest.

Gerda sat at the old woman's table and nibbled cherries while she told her all about Kay and how she was setting out to find him. The old woman nodded and smiled and took out a comb from her pocket. "How long I've waited for a pretty little girl like you!" she exclaimed as she began combing Gerda's silky yellow hair. The more she combed, the more Gerda forgot about her home and the search for Kay, for the woman was an enchantress, and her comb was a magical one.

That night, while Gerda was asleep, the old woman went out into her garden. She pulled her magic comb out of her pocket and it turned into a magic wand.

She waved the wand over her rose bushes and they immediately sank into the ground, leaving not a trace behind. The old woman did not want Gerda to be reminded of the roses at home, but to forget completely and live in the cottage with her forever.

Many days passed and Gerda spent her time playing in the garden. The old woman's flowers were magical too, each with a story to tell. Gerda loved to listen to them, yet when they had finished she always felt as though something was missing.

One morning, the old woman left her sunbonnet on the table and Gerda picked it up to examine the flowers embroidered on it. As she turned the brim in her hands, she caught sight of a beautiful pink rose. Suddenly, a picture of the rose arch at home flashed into her mind, and she saw herself sitting there with Kay as they had done so many times before.

Gerda jumped to her feet in horror at having forgotten her promise to find Kay and bring him home. She ran out of the cottage, down the path and through the gate.

As she ran, Gerda saw that the leaves were falling from the trees and there were bright red and orange berries on the bushes. It was autumn, she realized with a shock. It had always been spring in the old woman's garden, so she hadn't noticed time passing. Now everything looked bleak and cold. "How much time I've wasted!" she cried. "What can have become of poor Kay!"

CHAPTER FOUR

The Prince and Princess

As Gerda was wondering what to do, a large black raven hopped across her path. He cocked his head on one side and fixed her with his black beady eye. "Where are you going, all alone?" he asked.

Gerda felt a lump come into her throat, but she swallowed hard and explained her quest to the raven. "Did Kay come this way? Have you seen him?" she finished anxiously.

The raven extended the claws of one foot and scratched in the soil. "I may have," he replied slowly.

Gerda trembled with excitement. "Take me to him?" she pleaded.

The raven looked very doubtful. "There is something you need to know," he said. "Kay, if it is he, is to marry a princess, and she is as clever as she is beautiful."

"No matter," answered Gerda earnestly. "I just want to see for myself that he is safe and happy."

The raven was touched by her sincerity and confided to her that his own beloved was a palace raven. "Wait here," he instructed, "and I shall fly to her, as she will doubtless know what to do and how it may be accomplished."

The raven flew off and Gerda sat down to wait. The tired girl soon fell fast asleep and when she woke up, it was evening and the raven had returned. "My beloved has agreed to meet us," he informed her. "She will take us to the royal bedchamber via a back staircase that is rarely guarded."

Gerda jumped to her feet. As she hurried after the raven, he told her about the princess and how unusual she was. She loved learning, he explained, spending her time in the royal library among

thousands of books. She was interested in marriage only if she found a man who equalled her in wit. Many suitors had tried to court her but none had been successful. None, that is, until one day a fair-haired boy had walked straight past all the guards and courtiers and announced: "I have not come to woo the princess, but to learn from her wisdom."

"That must have been Kay," Gerda thought when she heard this. "He is always so brave and clever."

At last a grand building appeared in the distance. When they reached it, they found a half-open door at the back and not a guard in sight. Gerda's heart was beating violently as they tiptoed inside. At the top of the stairs was perched an elegant female raven. Gerda curtsied and the raven nodded regally in reply. "Your quest is a worthy one and close to my heart," she said. "Pick up the lamp, my dear."

As they passed through large rooms hung with silks and satins in every hue, Gerda was startled by huge black shadows rustling and whispering along the walls. There were knights and ladies, horses and castles, and other shapes and figures, too many to count and constantly changing.

"These are dreams," explained the raven softly, "they are here to entertain the lords and ladies while they sleep."

Then they came to the very last room, in which stood a great golden pillar. Looking up, Gerda saw that it was the trunk of a huge tree, its shining branches stretching up to form the ceiling and the facets of its graceful glass leaves twinkling in the lamplight. From the tree hung two beds in the shape of lilies, one white and one red. In the white bed slept the princess and in the red one slept the boy.

Gerda climbed up to the boy's bed and shone the lamp on his hair. She whispered his name and he awoke. Dismay poured through her, for it wasn't Kay.

The princess had woken up too, by this time, and she and the prince listened intently while the ravens recounted Gerda's story. They were impressed by Gerda's courage and persuaded her to stay the night.

As she slept, shadowy dream figures flitted around her. She saw angels pulling sledges and Kay smiling and waving to her. When she awoke, the pictures vanished but her resolve had been strengthened and she was more determined than ever to continue her quest.

In return for all the help they had given Gerda, the princess offered the two ravens positions at court with rights to all the leftover food from the palace kitchens. The ravens accepted gratefully, overjoyed to be together at last. The prince and princess begged Gerda to stay awhile at the palace, but all she asked for was a horse so that she could be on her way. "Of course!" declared the princess. "And you must be properly dressed for the journey." She provided Gerda with an immaculate velvet riding coat, trimmed with fur and with leather buttons. "Now," she said, "let us find you a mount."

They walked over to the stables, the princess inviting Gerda to choose from a range of magnificent horses from every corner of the globe. Gerda stopped in front of each of them and asked, "Have you seen my friend Kay?" But none of them had seen or heard of him. Then she came to a stall where a handsome reindeer was waiting. "I have not met the boy you speak of," he said in a grave voice, "but I can feel your suffering, for I too have lost a very dear friend. Climb on my back; I will help you."

One of the palace grooms saddled and bridled the reindeer, hanging sacks of delicious food and wine along his flanks. "Good-bye and good luck!" cried the prince and princess.

Gerda thanked them warmly and waved good-bye. The raven volunteered to be her guide once more, flying above her as she set out again along the banks of the fast-flowing river.

The Outlaw Girl

Before long, they entered a dark forest where the heavily laden reindeer drew the eyes of the forest outlaws, who sprang out of the undergrowth and seized him by the bridle. The bags of provisions were taken and Gerda was dragged from the saddle. Her arms were pinned behind her back, and a bony robber with bristling eyebrows and a hairy chin prodded and poked at her new clothes. "Quite the little lady…" he murmured as he drew his sharp dagger and held it to her throat.

"No!" shouted a clear, commanding young voice. "She shall give me her fine clothes but you won't hurt her as she shall be my friend." Looking up, Gerda saw a young outlaw girl with tangled hair jump onto the man's back and bite him fiercely. The robber grimaced

with pain and the girl leapt into the reindeer's saddle, pulling Gerda up behind her. "We shall ride home in comfort!" she declared as the outlaws stepped out of the way. "Don't be afraid," she added to Gerda. "Father won't kill you so long as I'm fond of you, not even if we should quarrel, for then I would rather do it myself."

Gerda could take little comfort from these words, nor from the gloomy, broken-down castle where they finally halted. Inside it was dark and full of smoke from the large fire where hares and rabbits were roasting on a great spit.

"Come and see my pets!" invited the girl, and she took Gerda to a corner of the room, where a sad-looking wolf was tied to a stake by a rope around his neck. Close by, some owls were hooting dismally in a makeshift cage constructed from twigs and brambles.

"Poor things!" exclaimed Gerda softly, feeling like a captive herself. "Why don't you let them go?"

The girl frowned. "Because then they'd fly away and leave me!" she replied.

"Hoo-hoo!" cried the owls. "We
would visit you every day! We would love
you because you had given us back our freedom."

The outlaw girl seemed lost in thought for a
moment and then she asked Gerda to tell her how
she came to be traveling through the forest.
Gerda told the story of Kay and her
resolve to find him. "But I don't
know where to look!" she
finished, despairingly.

"Hoo-hoo! We do!" cried the owls. "The Snow Queen has whirled him away to her palace in the North."

"How do you know that?" asked Gerda.

"They flew past us on a sleigh pulled by big white birds," answered the owls sadly, "and as they passed by, the Snow Queen leaned over and blew her frosty breath on our fledglings and they died."

Gerda felt a chill strike her heart and she determined to be on her way as soon as possible. "Can you tell me how to find her palace?" she pleaded.

"You must speak to the wolf," said one owl. "He knows those lands."

Then the wolf, who had been listening quietly, spoke up. "The Snow Queen lives far, far away in the North, your way lies across many miles of snow and ice."

"Oh no!" cried Gerda. "Kay, I will *never* find you!"

"You can't just give up!" hissed the outlaw girl. "There must be a way." She turned to the wolf. "Do you know how to get there?"

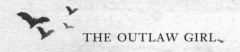

"Of course," replied the wolf proudly. "I was born there."

"Very well," said the girl. "The men will be out hunting tonight and I can take care of my mother. Be ready to leave when I give the word."

In the early hours of the morning, when all was still and quiet, the outlaw girl shook her mother awake and gave her a flask of rum. The woman drank it all and was soon sound asleep again. Next, the girl gave Gerda a shake.

CHAPTER FIVE

"There's no time to lose!" she whispered. "Kay needs you." She threw a cloak around Gerda's shoulders, handed her a bundle of food and led her to the wolf. "He will take you to the Snow Queen's palace," she said, slipping the rope from the wolf's neck.

They crept quietly out of the castle, the wolf's eyes gleaming with excitement at being freed at last. The outlaw girl helped Gerda onto the reindeer's back. "Here is some cheese and brandy to keep you going," she said. Then she turned to the raven, the wolf and the reindeer. "Take good care of her!" she commanded. "Or you'll feel the lash of my whip!"

The wolf raised his head and sniffed the air. Then, with the scent of home in his nostrils, he set off through the wood, with his muzzle turned to the North. The reindeer galloped behind, and the raven flew above them. They journeyed on in the moonlight, through great forests and wide open spaces. Every so often, other wolves could be heard howling in the distance, and the air grew colder and colder the further north they traveled. Gerda pulled her cloak tighter around her and wriggled her numb toes. The air grew colder still until they were passing through vast tracts of snow while the stars glittered overhead. Suddenly, the wolf stopped. "Are we there yet?" Gerda asked sleepily and looking up, she rubbed her eyes in astonishment. In the sky were the most beautiful colors — crimson, violet, blue and emerald — constantly changing and forming different patterns. "Oh!" she cried with joy. "Is this magic?"

"It is the Northern Lights," said the wolf proudly. "Now I know I am home again." And they went on faster than ever, until at last they came to Lapland. Here, the wolf stopped at a little hut set in an open expanse of snow.

CHAPTER SIX

The Wise Woman of the North

"Who lives here?" Gerda asked fearfully as she slid off the reindeer's back.

"The Wise Woman," answered the wolf, and at that moment, the door of the hut opened and a delicious smell of cooking filled the night air. Gerda's stomach rumbled and she remembered how long it had been since she had last eaten. She stepped inside.

It was quite dark in the hut except for the light of the fire, over which hung a large cooking pot. Gerda could just make out a dark shape bent over the pot, stirring it with a spoon. She hung back a little, but the wolf pushed past and the shape revealed itself to be an old woman with grey plaits, dressed in padded sealskin.

She stroked the wolf and called him by a name in his own language, then she turned to Gerda and handed her a bowl of hot soup. She produced a juicy bone for the wolf, lichen for the reindeer, and for the raven a tasty anchovy. For a while all was quiet in the hut except for the clinking of Gerda's spoon, the munching sounds from the animals and the crackle of the fire.

Then the wolf spoke. "Wise Woman," he said eagerly, "can you give Gerda a potion? Or some magical talisman that will endow her with the strength of twelve men so that she can defeat the Snow Queen?"

The Wise Woman smiled and shook her head. "I can give her nothing so powerful as that which she already has — a loving heart." The wolf looked downcast and Gerda felt disappointed. Now that she was so close to the Snow Queen's palace she realized that she had not yet thought of a plan to rescue Kay.

Tired from their travels, Gerda and her three companions soon fell asleep while the Wise Woman tended the fire and watched over them.

The next day, the four friends set off on the last part of their journey. A few snowflakes started to fall and the wolf began to tremble. After a while, the reindeer drew to a halt. "This is the beginning of the Snow Queen's territory," he said. "I feel her power growing and I cannot go with you any further." The wolf and the raven could also go no further.

Gerda thanked her friends for all their help and bid them a sad good-bye. As she stroked the wolf's thick fur, a single tear rolled down his face. "We will wait here for you, Gerda," said the raven. "Farewell and good luck."

Gerda tucked her cloak around her and set off bravely into the cold north wind. As she trudged through the snow, the wind blew more fiercely, with a wild, keening sound, and the snowflakes fell more thickly. Suddenly, she noticed that that the snowflakes were no longer falling from the sky but traveling horizontally across the ground. They took on menacing forms: huge porcupines, knotted snakes and great bears.

An army of them was closing in on her. Gerda kept pushing forwards and began to pray with all her might. It was so cold that her breath turned to ice vapor and floated right up into the sky. As she watched, the vapor became a legion of bright angels who glided to the ground, forming a safe wall around her. Each angel wore a helmet, shield and spear, which they used to shatter the snowflake army into tiny pieces.

Gerda kept on walking, unafraid now and no longer feeling the bitter cold because the angels had brought warmth to her hands and feet.

At long last, Gerda came to an enormous staircase made entirely of ice. Step by step, she climbed up the stairs.

Higher and higher she climbed, determined to reach Kay and free him from his icy prison.

CHAPTER SEVEN

The Snow Queen's Palace

And what of Kay — how had he fared in the Snow Queen's palace all this time? There was no warmth within its snowy halls. Even the Northern Lights, which lit its vast empty spaces, offered no warmth but seemed to glow in a cold, dreamlike manner. No one laughed here and no company or fun was to be had. When the Snow Queen was in residence, she sat in state in the middle of a frozen lake. She called it her mirror of reason and was proud of the fact that it was the only one in the world. Kay sat at her feet, busy constructing jigsaws from icy fragments. The complex symmetrical patterns that he made were a wonder to behold. Sometimes he made words but there was one word that he could never form, and that was eternity. 'When you can make that word, you

will be a free man,' promised the Snow Queen. "Indeed, I will give you the whole world and a new pair of skates into the bargain!" But however hard he tried, Kay never succeeded.

"Now, I must visit some warm countries," said the Snow Queen. "I shall fly above their volcanoes and make a little snow fall into them in order to finish off the grape and lemon harvests." And away she flew, leaving Kay alone with his puzzles.

Gerda, meanwhile, was nearing her goal. Holding her hand up to shield her eyes from the brightness, she could just see the sparkling walls of the palace, made entirely of ice and frost. The gates swung open to let her enter. She walked along passageways lit by the Northern Lights until she came out into a courtyard. In its center was the dazzling frozen lake and, in the middle of the ice, sat a lonely figure. It was Kay, trying as ever to piece together some shards of ice to form a word. Over and over again he assembled and reassembled the letters, but they made no sense.

Gerda's heart leapt when she saw Kay after such a long, long time. She called out to him but he did not seem to hear her. Unsteadily, she ventured out across the slippery ice until she came to the place where he was sitting. "Kay — it's me, Gerda!" she cried. "I have come to take you home." Kay looked at her with dull, uncomprehending eyes. He was stiff and silent, blue with cold. Gerda thought her heart would break. She threw her arms around Kay's neck and sobbed bitterly. What if he did not want to come home, after all? Little did she know but her hot, salty tears were melting the ice in his heart and, with it, the splinter of glass at its core.

Slowly, Kay looked around him. All at once, he recognized Gerda. He wept for joy and the splinter of glass in his eye floated away with his tears. Gerda saw the color flow back into his cheeks. Looking down, Kay noticed that the shards of ice had formed themselves into a word, the very word that he had been trying to make all this time. In sparkling letters, they spelled out:

E-T-E-R-N-I-T-Y.

He smiled through his tears and hugged Gerda tightly. He was free at last!

Just at that happy moment, the Snow Queen appeared. Her stare was so icy that Gerda felt frost beginning to form on her eyelashes, but she blinked and stared bravely back. "*You!*" hissed the Snow Queen. "How dare you enter my palace? I'll turn you into a block of ice!"

"You will not," said Gerda stoutly. "You cannot!"

"What?" thundered the Snow Queen, and the sound of a thousand avalanches was in her voice.

Gerda remembered the Wise Woman. "I have a loving heart," she stammered, "and you — you have no heart at all! Everyone here is frozen with misery, but I have brought the color back to Kay's cheeks and washed away the splinter of glass from his heart with my warm tears."

The Snow Queen spun round and looked at Kay. It was true his heart was no longer frozen. She gave a loud cry like the sound of thick ice groaning and splitting on a frozen lake. Her beautiful face began to crack and splinter and in a second she had shattered into a thousand ice crystals that were whirled away by the wind.

Gerda kissed Kay's hands for joy and the two friends ran away down the corridors and out through the gates into the glorious sunshine and blue skies of a bright winter's day. There they found the Snow Queen's sleigh, with a white reindeer harnessed to it.

"Quick!" called the reindeer. "Climb on board! You have saved me from a terrible fate; I should like to repay the favor."

Away they sped — and they were not a moment too soon. As the sleigh flew across the ice, there was a terrible cracking sound and the whole of the Snow Queen's palace sank into the icy, northern sea with a deafening roar. The sleigh came to a halt outside the Wise Woman's hut, where Gerda's friends were waiting for her. The wolf howled with pleasure when he saw Kay with Gerda. As for the reindeer, he recognized his lost friend straight away and would not leave her side.

When they had eaten and rested and Kay's clothes were dry once more, the Wise Woman blessed them all and the little party set off again. This time the way seemed so much easier. Gerda and Kay rode on the two reindeer and the wolf accompanied them to the border of their own country. There they parted and Gerda promised to visit him again someday at the Wise Woman's hut in the northern lands. At the mention of his beloved home, the wolf pricked up his ears and he was eager to be off. Kay and Gerda waved good-bye until he disappeared over the horizon.

Their way home lay through rugged hills and valleys, but they did not mind as it was sweet to have each other for company once again. Suddenly the bushes parted to reveal a young girl riding a fine horse. Gerda recognized the rider as the outlaw girl and wondered if the horse had been stolen from a passing traveler. They greeted each other with surprise and pleasure and Gerda introduced Kay. The outlaw girl looked him up and down. "Well," she said, "so you are the young man that this brave girl risked life and limb to rescue!"

Gerda asked for news of the prince and princess. "Their royal highnesses are traveling in foreign lands, but tell me, how was it that you found each other again?" And Gerda and Kay told their story with all its twists and turns while the outlaw girl listened intently, shaking her head in amazement. She promised to visit them if she ever passed through their town and, turning her horse around, she rode away to see the world.

As they drew closer to home, the two friends noticed that the trees were in leaf and the flowers were blooming. The sun was warm on their backs and the air was mild. When they came to the walls of their town, they said good-bye to the two reindeer and the faithful raven, who was anxious to return to his beloved. Kay and Gerda embraced their friends and walked on through the gates. As they did so, all the church bells rang out to welcome them home. When they reached their own street, they saw that the rose trees were once more in bud and they stopped to admire the arch that joined their two houses.

As their families ran out to greet them, Kay and Gerda realized that they were now as tall as their parents. Several years must have passed while they were away. They were children no longer, and a beautiful spring world was waiting for them.

Barefoot Books
2067 Massachusetts Ave
Cambridge, MA 02140

Adapted from the fairy tale by Hans Christian Andersen
Text copyright © 2011 by Sarah Lowes
Illustrations by Miss Clara, first published in France as
La Reine des glaces © Hachette-Livre / Gautier-Languereau, 2010
The moral rights of Sarah Lowes and Miss Clara have been asserted
Story CD narrated by Xanthe Gresham
Recorded, mixed and mastered by Sans Walk Spoken Word Studio, England

First published in the United States of America by Barefoot Books, Inc in 2011
This hardback edition with story CD first published in 2013

Graphic design by Louise Millar, London
Color separation by B&P International, Hong Kong
Printed in China on 100% acid-free paper
This book was typeset in Filosofia, Azola and Janson
The illustrations were prepared as scale models,
which were photographed and digitally enhanced

ISBN: 978-1-84686-964-8

Library of Congress Cataloging-in-Publication Data
is available under 2011006903

1 3 5 7 9 8 6 4 2